10-19-91

To Sun, Andy,
Claire, Lauren,
Sara

Why do shrews sing the Blues
In high-heeled Tennis shoes?

BECAUSE . . .
when they sing them in loafers
they turn into gophers.

Read Parsley

R

Meet the Shrews

Meet the Shrews

WORDS BY

REED PARSLEY

PICTURES BY

SPARKY FOX

GREEN TIGER PRESS

Published by Simon & Schuster

New York London Toronto Sydney Tokyo Singapore

This is how it all began ... with one young shrew, a shrew named Johnny, sitting by the railroad tracks on a cold moonlit night, dreaming an age-old dream. Alone he sat, just he and his horn, and there was music in the firelight.

A great idea was born the night Johnny Shrew opened up his heart to his best friend, Sid Shrew. They met at the old mole hole where they strolled underground and spoke of their shared dream:

"The world needs our music, Sid, for it's true we shrews have soul."

"As you know, I feel the same as you, Johnny, so let's go show them what we can do!"

Johnny and Sid packed up their modest belongings and headed for the Shrew Mission District on the outskirts of town.

Said Johnny, "I know two of the coolest shrews who live here. Their names are Buddy and Lou, and I know they'll join us if we ask them, for they, too, want a music career."

So the four shrews, Johnny, Sid, Buddy and Lou, rented a bus and hit the road, Jack. They drove for four days and four nights.

On the fourth night they stopped, having no idea where they were until a shrew who seemed to be expecting them waved and shouted, "Welcome to Chicago!"

Of course, no one had ever heard of this new shrew
band. But Johnny and the boys didn't care where they
played or who heard them. They set up a stage in a
back alley on the south side.

   Street mice gathered around to listen into the wee
hours. They could hardly believe their ears! After all,
what mouse had ever known even one shrew who could
play classic Rat-Scat jazz?

Word quickly got around about Johnny and his
Blue-Shrew Boys. They were invited to play indoors
before a packed house during a free concert at Chicago's
Convention Center.

Johnny and Sid blew trumpet; Buddy blew tenor
sax. They blew cool jazz in their platform sneakers,
while Lou sneaked off for some snacks.

Then came the big break everyone had hoped for. A producer for RRR (Rockin' Rodent Records) gave Johnny and his Blue-Shrew Boys a recording session at a famous studio where they cut a brilliant demo tape.

They sang soprano, alto, tenor, bass; shrews in four parts at an R&B pace.

Upon hearing the demo tape, a rich pygmy shrew booked Johnny and the boys on a Caribbean cruise. For payment, he gave each of them a year's supply of high-heeled tennis shoes and all the buffet grubs they could eat.

As they became ever more popular, Johnny and his
Blue-Shrew Boys played more and more club dates at
better and better places.

They doo-wopped and bopped late into each night.
This fabulous foursome the crowds did delight.

They blew 'em away, four shrews with true class; when they hit all the high notes, they blew out the glass!

Soon Johnny and the boys made all the headlines that sold the news. They became America's favorite ambassadors of blues.

Suddenly, the Shrews were in demand all over the globe. They embarked on a world-wide barnstorming tour.

Adoring fans in London flung tennis shoes on stage, where Johnny and his high-heeled rogues had all become the rage.

They stopped next in Germany, not knowing where to begin. They jammed in all the cabarets, then vamped in East Berlin.

They did a quick spin across South America where Brazilian nuts flipped for their cool jazz.

Then it was on to Mother Russia, comrades, to dance the Razz-ma-tazz!

Bravely they stormed into France, where no one gave them much of a chance.

In Paris, they found a high-fashion groove. The French went wild when they played the Louvre.

Back in America, when the tour had ended, the Blue-Shrew Boys were bushed. "I'm exhausted," said Sid. "I'm so beat, I can't eat," said Lou. "I can hardly believe what's happened to us," said Buddy. "We've played our music all over the world! Our dream's come true; what's left to do?"

Just then, Johnny Shrew popped in. "Remember, lads, we still have to prove we're the number one band here in our own country. So pack up your sneakers, shrews. We're set to open in two days as the featured attraction in ..."

LAS VEGAS!"

And that's exactly what happened. Johnny and the boys became the main headliners at their own High-Top Hotel. Hip people from all over the world came to hole-up and hear the Shrews belt the blues in their flashy new digs.

And that's where they remain to this very day. So, if you're planning to go hear the hottest shrews ever to sing the blues in their own high-rise, high-heeled tennis shoes, be sure to call first. Space is tight, and reservations are highly recommended.

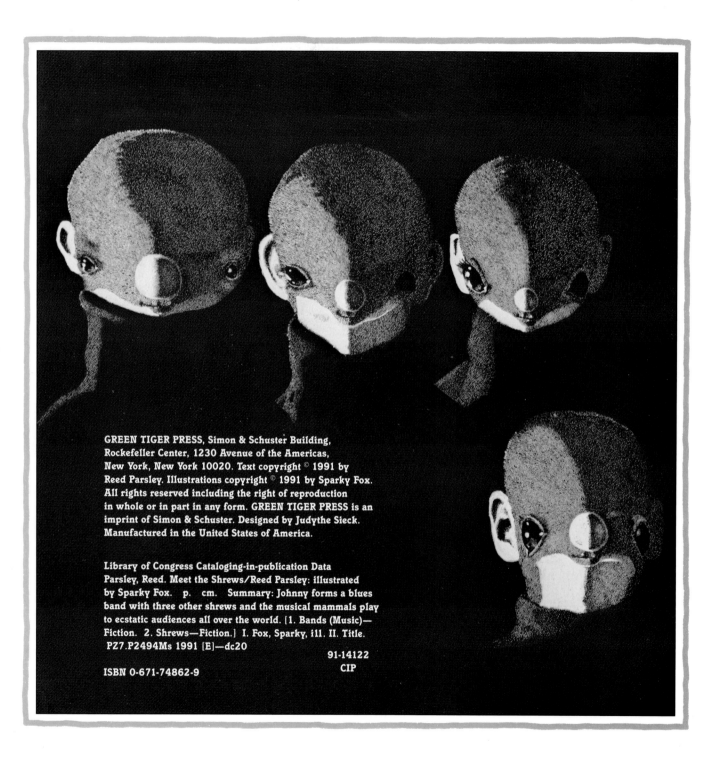

GREEN TIGER PRESS, Simon & Schuster Building,
Rockefeller Center, 1230 Avenue of the Americas,
New York, New York 10020. Text copyright © 1991 by
Reed Parsley. Illustrations copyright © 1991 by Sparky Fox.
All rights reserved including the right of reproduction
in whole or in part in any form. GREEN TIGER PRESS is an
imprint of Simon & Schuster. Designed by Judythe Sieck.
Manufactured in the United States of America.

Library of Congress Cataloging-in-publication Data
Parsley, Reed. Meet the Shrews/Reed Parsley: illustrated
by Sparky Fox. p. cm. Summary: Johnny forms a blues
band with three other shrews and the musical mammals play
to ecstatic audiences all over the world. [1. Bands (Music)—
Fiction. 2. Shrews—Fiction.] I. Fox, Sparky, ill. II. Title.
PZ7.P2494Ms 1991 [E]—dc20
                                    91-14122
                                    CIP
ISBN 0-671-74862-9